The Last Ember

The last man's legacy

Susnata Mondal

ISBN 978-93-5883-045-3
© Susnata Mondal 2023

Published in India 2023 by Pencil

A brand of

One Point Six Technologies Pvt. Ltd.
Unit no. 26, Ground Floor, Building A1,
Wadala Truck Terminal Road,
Near Post Office, Antop Hill, Mumbai - 400037
E connect@thepencilapp.com
W www.thepencilapp.com

Author biography

Hello, dear readers! I am Susnata Mondal, and I am thrilled to have you join me on my literary journey where words come alive. This is a place where I unleash my creativity, share my thoughts, and connect with a community of like-minded individuals.

Through the power of the written word, I aim to inspire, educate, and entertain.

CONTENTS

Preface

Looking for an idea for a book, I turned to my friend Rishav Chowdhury, in December, 2022. From him I got the idea for this book. I had just finished writing and publishing my debut book,"Perfect Life" in October, 2022. I wanted to take a break before starting something new. So, I put it aside and decided to start writing A month later. Fast forward to April of 2023, and I finally started with this story. To be honest, this was the fastest I have ever worked. And there is no specific reason for it. The first draft of this work was compiled in a very short span of a month. Editing and proofreading took some more time, perhaps another month. The final copy was then tossed back into the drawer as I got busy again. Finally, in July of this year(2023), I had the time to sit down to revise and publish it.

Hope you enjoy!

Regards,
Susnata Mondal

Acknowledgements

I would like to express my deepest gratitude and appreciation to all those who have contributed to the creation and completion of this book. Without their support, guidance, and encouragement, this project would not have been possible.

First and foremost, I would like to thank my family for their unwavering love, understanding, and belief in me throughout this journey. Their constant encouragement and support have been the driving force behind my pursuit of knowledge and the completion of this book.

I extend my heartfelt thanks to my supervisor, Mr. Suvro Chatterjee, for his invaluable guidance, expertise, and encouragement. Their insightful feedback and constructive criticism have played a pivotal role in shaping the content and structure of this book.

I would like to acknowledge the contributions of Rishav Chowdhury, and Vighnesh Goswami, who provided assistance in various stages of the book's development. Their input, suggestions, and meticulous proofreading have significantly improved the clarity and quality of the final manuscript.

I would also like to express my gratitude to my friends who have been a constant source of inspiration and motivation. Their support, intellectual discussions, and willingness to lend an ear have been invaluable during the writing process.

Last but not least, I want to thank my readers for their interest and support. Your enthusiasm and engagement with the ideas presented in this book have been incredibly motivating and rewarding.In conclusion, I am humbled and grateful to all those who have played a part in bringing this book to life. Your contributions, whether big or small, have left an indelible mark on this work. Thank you for believing in me and for being a part of this incredible journey.

Sincerely,
Susnata Mondal

Sincerely,Susnata Mondal

Good morning

I opened my eyes, my body heavy with sleep. The room was shrouded in darkness, and for a moment, I lay still, disoriented. Slowly, my surroundings materialised as my senses sharpened. The faint glow of moonlight seeped through the tattered curtains, casting ethereal shadows across the walls. The air felt stale, as if time itself had come to a standstill.

I pushed myself up, the worn mattress creaking beneath my weight. The sensation of cold linoleum met my bare feet as they made contact with the floor. A shiver coursed through my body, and I glanced around, expecting familiarity, seeking the comforting presence of my loved ones. But there was nothing.

"Hello?" I called out, my voice a mere whisper, as if afraid to disturb the fragile silence that engulfed me. The echo of my own voice filled the void, a haunting reminder of the emptiness that surrounded me. Panic began to claw its way up my throat, my heartbeat pounding in my ears.

I stumbled out of bed, my steps unsteady as I navigated the dimly lit room. Shadows danced on the walls, casting eerie shapes that seemed to mock my confusion. My hands reached out, searching for something tangible, a connection to reality. But all I found was emptiness.

With trembling hands, I pushed open the bedroom door, and a chill seeped into my bones as I entered the hallway.

The house was enveloped in an eerie stillness, devoid of the usual signs of life. No sounds of laughter, no familiar footsteps echoing through the halls. My voice cracked as I called out again, desperate for a response that never came.

The front door swung open with a creek, and I stepped outside, hoping to find answers in the world beyond. The moon hung high in the sky, casting a pale glow on the abandoned street. My footsteps echoed through the silence as I wandered through the empty neighbourhood, my eyes scanning for any signs of life.

The houses stood like sentinels, their windows shattered their doors ajar, as if they had witnessed a cataclysmic event. I peered into each empty home, the remnants of lives once lived staring back at me—a child's toy left abandoned, a half-empty coffee mug frozen in time. They whispered tales of a vanished world, amplifying the hollow ache in my chest.

Time seemed to blur as I walked, my mind filled with questions that had no answers. How had this come to be? Where has everyone gone? I gazed up at the night sky, its vastness a stark reminder of my insignificance, as if the universe itself was indifferent to my existence.

Hours turned into an eternity as I continued my search, my footsteps the only sound punctuating the silence. The park, once teeming with laughter and playful voices, now lay deserted, the swings swaying gently in the breeze as if beckoning to a world that no longer existed.

Exhaustion weighed heavily upon me, my body weary from the fruitless quest for companionship. I returned home, the solitude pressing against my soul like a suffocating veil. The walls seemed to close in around me; the hollowness of the house magnified in the absence of laughter and shared memories.

I collapsed onto the worn couch, my mind swirling with a mix of despair and disbelief. I yearned for the comfort of human presence, for the sound of familiar voices that had vanished without a trace. I closed my eyes, seeking solace in the darkness, hoping that tomorrow would bring answers, that somehow, in this empty world, I would find a purpose to carry on.

Am I alone

Days turned into weeks, and weeks stretched into months, as I navigated the labyrinth of my solitary existence. The silence had become my constant companion, an unyielding presence that followed me wherever I went. Time lost its meaning, blending into a seamless continuum of isolated moments.

Within the confines of my empty home, I established a fragile routine, a feeble attempt to retain some semblance of normalcy. Mornings were greeted with the weak rays of sunlight that filtered through the cracked windows, casting pale streaks of illumination on the faded wallpaper. I would rise from my bed, aching muscles protesting against the weight of desolation, and embark on the rituals of survival.

With measured steps, I moved through the rooms, each one holding memories that threatened to consume me. I dusted the forgotten surfaces, their accumulation of neglect serving as a physical manifestation of the absence of life. The sound of my own breathing seemed amplified, filling the void left by the absence of human interaction.

Necessity became my guide as I scoured the abandoned remnants of the neighbourhood, searching for supplies to sustain me in this desolate landscape. The grocery store shelves once brim with a myriad of choices, now stood barren and haunting, a stark reflection of the barrenness that had taken hold of my existence.

I gathered canned goods and non-perishables, clinging to the hope that sustenance would continue to accompany me on this solitary journey. Water, a precious resource, was carefully rationed, its scarcity a constant reminder of the fragility of survival.

My home, once a sanctuary of shared joys and sorrows, now stood as a monument to the silence. I found solace in the familiar spaces, the creaking floorboards beneath my feet, and the faded photographs on the walls. They became my companions, their silent gazes a reminder of the world that had faded away.

As the seasons shifted, nature began to reclaim what was once hers. Overgrown vines crept through cracks in the pavement, determined to reclaim their territory. I marvelled at the resilience of the wild, the persistence of life even in the absence of human touch. In the garden that I cultivated, nurtured sprouts that broke through the earth's surface, their tender shoots, a testament to the enduring spirit of growth.

The loneliness that enveloped me, like a fog that refused to dissipate, was met with resistance. I sought refuge in the pages of books, their stories transporting me to worlds far beyond the desolation that surrounded me. In the written words, I found solace and a temporary reprieve from my solitary existence.

Days blended together, and the boundaries between waking and dreaming blurred. Dreams became my escape, an alternate reality where I could once again embrace loved ones, laugh with friends, and be part of a world that was slowly fading from memory. But as I awoke each morning, the dreams slipped away, leaving me grasping at fading fragments of joy.

The nights were the hardest to endure. The darkness that settled upon the land seemed to amplify the weight of my isolation. The silence became deafening, punctuated only by the distant howling of the wind. I lay awake, my thoughts echoing through the empty chambers of my mind, contemplating the meaning of my existence in this desolate world.

Yet, amidst the overwhelming solitude, a quiet resilience blossomed within me. I embraced the stillness, allowing it to seep into my soul. I found solace in the beauty of a sunset that painted the sky with fiery hues, in the gentle breeze that caressed my skin, and in the stars that twinkle in the vast expanse above.

In this world bereft of human companionship, I had discovered a new kinship with nature. I observed the delicate dance of the butterflies, the graceful flight of birds, and the symphony of insects that carried on their eternal conversations. A stray dog, battered and alone, crossed my path one day, and with hesitant steps, it joined me on this journey of solitude, our shared loneliness bridging the void that separated us.

I would explore the remnants of the city, accompanied by the loyal canine companion by my side. We would traverse the deserted streets, marvelling at the way nature had begun to reclaim the crumbling buildings and asphalt. It was as if the earth herself was attempting to heal the scars left by the absence of humanity.

As I watched the dog chase its tail in playful abandon, a spark of joy ignited within me. In the simplicity of these moments, I realised that even in the absence of human companionship, life still had the capacity to bloom. In the company of nature, and the loyal presence of my canine friend, I embarked on a slow-paced journey of acceptance, finding solace in the echoes of solitude that surrounded me.

The past echoes before me

The days melded into one another, a seamless tapestry of routine and solitude. The presence of my loyal canine companion brought a measure of warmth to my isolated existence. Together, we traversed the abandoned streets, our footfalls breaking the stillness that hung heavy in the air.

In our explorations, we stumbled upon remnants of the past that whispered tales of a forgotten civilization. I discovered a weathered bookstore, its shelves lined with forgotten knowledge, its scent of aged paper and ink permeating the air. Books became my refuge, portals to distant worlds, and companions in my solitude. I would spend hours immersed in their pages, finding solace in the words of writers long gone, their stories weaving a delicate thread between the past and my present reality.

One afternoon, as I roamed the empty city, I stumbled upon a neglected art gallery. Paintings adorned the walls, frozen in time; their vibrant colours, a stark contrast to the desolation that surrounded me. I stood before each canvas, allowing myself to be consumed by the emotions they evoked. In the strokes of a brush, I found echoes of human expression, a connection to the creative spirit that once thrived.

The artwork became my companions, their frozen scenes telling stories that only the eyes could comprehend. I would sit for hours, absorbing their beauty, losing myself in the details, and imagining the artists who had breathed life into each stroke. Their presence lingered, bridging the gap between the past and my solitary present.

As time passed, my relationship with the dog deepened. It became my confidant, its eyes filled with a wisdom that transcended words. In its presence, I found comfort and a sense of companionship, a reminder that even in the absence of human connection, the bonds between living beings could endure.

The seasons continued to change, painting the world in ever-changing hues. I witnessed the delicate blossoming of spring flowers, the vibrant foliage of summer, the fiery palette of autumn, and the stark beauty of winter's embrace. Each season carried its own poetry, a reminder that life, in all its forms, was a relentless force.

In the evenings, as the sun dipped below the horizon, I would sit by a crackling fire, its warmth enveloping me, warding off the chill of solitude. I would lose myself in the dancing flames, their flickering light casting a soft glow on the worn walls of my home. The crackling embers whispered secrets, offering a semblance of connection to the world that had faded away.

With time, my yearning for human contact began to transform. I realised that solitude could be a canvas upon which I could paint my own existence. I delved into forgotten hobbies, embracing the creative spirit that had slumbered within me. I painted, wrote, and crafted, pouring my thoughts and emotions into tangible forms of expression. The empty rooms of my home became a sanctuary of creativity, each piece a testament to the resilience of the human spirit.

As I embraced my newfound solitude, I found solace in the echoes of the past. The remnants of a forgotten world became a catalyst for self-discovery, for finding purpose within the void. And though the absence of human companionship remained a constant ache, I learned to seek solace in the connections I had forged with nature, with art, and with the loyal presence of my canine companion.

In this slow-paced existence, I discovered that the echoes of the past held fragments of hope. They whispered stories of resilience and the enduring capacity of the human spirit. And so, with every step I took, I carried those echoes within me, a reminder that even in the vastness of solitude, life could still be lived, and its beauty could still be embraced.

Its all nice and slow

Time marched on relentlessly, its passage marked by the changing seasons and the gradual transformation of the post-apocalyptic world. The familiarity of routine had settled into the marrow of my existence, providing a semblance of stability amidst the desolation. But within the confines of my solitude, an undercurrent of curiosity began to stir.

The need to explore beyond the boundaries of my known surroundings grew stronger with each passing day. The lingering question of what lay beyond the borders of my deserted city gnawed at the corners of my consciousness. With a newfound sense of purpose, I embarked on a journey of discovery, guided by an insatiable desire to unravel the mysteries that shrouded the world.

Equipped with a backpack filled with provisions, a map scoured from the remnants of a library, and my loyal canine companion by my side, I set forth into the uncharted territories that lay beyond. We ventured into the untamed wilderness, where nature had triumphed in the absence of humanity.

The once-familiar landscapes gave way to unfamiliar vistas. Towering trees reached for the heavens, their branches entwined in a dance of life and resilience. Rivers flowed with a steadfast determination, their currents a testament to the enduring forces of nature. Mountains loomed in the distance, their peaks obscured by mist and mystery.

With each step, I marvelled at the beauty that had flourished in the absence of human interference. I revelled in the harmony of nature's symphony, the chirping of birds, the rustling of leaves, and the whispers of the wind weaving together in a delicate cacophony of sound. It was a world untouched, a sanctuary of serenity that held secrets waiting to be unveiled.

Days turned into weeks as we trekked through the wilderness, the map serving as our guide through the labyrinth of the unknown. We encountered remnants of human presence along the way—a dilapidated cabin, an overgrown trail, fragments of crumbling infrastructure. These scattered artefacts stood as monuments to a forgotten civilization, their stories left untold, their purpose now lost to time.

As we ventured deeper into the wilderness, a sense of awe mingled with trepidation. The sheer vastness of the untamed expanse overwhelmed me, reminding me of my own insignificance. Yet, an unyielding determination propelled me forward, the thirst for knowledge and connection fueling my every step.

In the midst of our exploration, we stumbled upon a hidden valley, nestled between towering peaks. It was a place untouched by the ravages of the cataclysm that had decimated the world. Lush greenery carpeted the ground, vibrant flowers bloomed in a riot of colours, and a crystal-clear stream meandered through the heart of the valley. It was a glimpse of paradise amidst the remnants of chaos.

In this secluded oasis, I discovered a community of wildlife, a microcosm of life flourishing in the absence of human presence. Deer grazed peacefully, rabbits darted through the undergrowth, and a symphony of birdsong filled the air. It was a reminder that life, in all its forms, would find a way to endure, even in the face of overwhelming loss.

Days turned into nights as I set up camp in this sanctuary, my tent nestled beneath the sheltering embrace of ancient trees. I would sit by the campfire, watching the stars emerge one by one, and their distant glow illuminating the vast expanse above. In the solitude of the night, I pondered the mysteries that still eluded me, wondering if I was truly the last person on Earth.

With each passing day, my connection to the natural world deepened. The vastness of the wilderness became a mirror for self-reflection, a canvas upon which I could trace the contours of my own existence. I discovered that the journey was not solely about unravelling the secrets of the external world, but also about delving into the depths of my own soul, peeling back the layers of fear, grief, and longing that had accumulated over time.

In this untamed wilderness, I found solace and a renewed sense of purpose. The unanswered questions that had plagued me became less important, replaced by a profound appreciation for the present moment. The world was no longer just a backdrop of desolation; it was a living, breathing entity that whispered stories of resilience, transformation, and the enduring spirit of life.

And so, in this chapter of my journey, I continued to traverse the unexplored expanses, guided by the allure of the unknown and fuelled by a sense of awe and wonder. The wilderness held its secrets close, teasing me with glimpses of hidden truths. With each step, I moved further into the depths of the unfathomable, eager to embrace whatever revelations the unfolding unknown had in store.

Echoes of Connection

As I delved deeper into the uncharted territories, my footsteps echoed with a newfound determination. The wilderness became my companion, its untamed beauty unfolding before me like a grand tapestry. The more I ventured into the unknown, the stronger my connection with the world grew, reminding me that I was never truly alone.

Amidst towering trees and meandering streams, I encountered other forms of life that had managed to survive the cataclysmic event. Families of squirrels chattered playfully in the treetops, while curious foxes observed my presence from a distance. Birds, with their melodic songs, serenaded me as I passed by, their colourful plumage a vibrant contrast against the green backdrop.

Nature, in all its diversity, embraced me as an observer and a participant. I observed the intricate dance of a spider weaving its delicate web, marvelled at the tenacity of wildflowers breaking through rocky soil, and bathed in the warmth of the sun as it filtered through the dense canopy above. These small moments of connection with the natural world became the threads that wove purpose into my journey.

As I continued my explorations, I stumbled upon a weathered cabin hidden amidst the wilderness. Its walls, worn by time and weather, stood as a testament to human presence in this forgotten realm. Intrigued, I cautiously approached, my heart filled with a mixture of trepidation and curiosity.

Inside, I discovered traces of a life that once thrived. The cabin, though abandoned, held remnants of memories—a worn armchair facing a cracked window, a faded photograph capturing a moment of joy, and a weathered journal with words etched upon its pages. It was a glimpse into the lives of those who had come before me, a reminder that I was not the first to traverse this post-apocalyptic world.

With bated breath, I turned the pages of the journal, eager to decipher the thoughts and experiences of its author. The words painted vivid pictures of survival, hope, and a longing for connection. They spoke of fears and dreams, of moments of despair and resilience. As I read, I felt a bond forming, an invisible thread connecting me to the writer, as if their words reached across time to touch my soul.

In the solitude of the cabin, I found solace. The journal became a bridge between past and present, allowing me to glimpse the lives that had intertwined with the world before it crumbled. Their stories reminded me that the human spirit, even in the face of unimaginable adversity, had the capacity to endure and seek solace in the simple joys of existence.

Empowered by this newfound connection, I embarked on a mission to uncover more remnants of humanity's presence. I journeyed to forgotten towns, exploring the remnants of once-bustling streets and decaying buildings. In each desolate corner, I discovered fragments of lives lived—a child's toy left behind, a faded mural on a brick wall, a handwritten letter tucked beneath floorboards.

These discoveries evoked a range of emotions within me—nostalgia, sorrow, and a deep appreciation for the fleeting nature of human existence. The remnants of a world that once was became a mosaic of stories, each fragment offering a glimpse into the collective tapestry of humanity.

Yet, even as I unearthed these echoes of the past, the truth of my solitude remained a constant companion. The absence of living souls lingered in the air, a reminder that the world had shifted, leaving me as the last witness to its transformation. And though I yearned for human connection, I began to realise that the true beauty of this journey lay not in finding others, but in the discoveries I made within myself. With the journal as my guide, I continued to seek solace in the natural world. I ventured to uncharted landscapes, climbed mountains that touched the heavens, and traversed sprawling plains that stretched as far as the eye could see. The wilderness became my sanctuary, its untamed spirit a mirror for my own untamed soul.

In the depths of solitude, I found a profound sense of freedom. The constraints of societal expectations and the burdens of a world left behind dissolved in the vastness of the wilderness. I learned to embrace the uncertainty and the ever-changing nature of my existence, finding strength in the resilience that had carried me thus far.

And so, in this chapter of my journey, I continued to tread upon the path less travelled. I embraced the echoes of connection—the stories of those who had come before me, the bonds formed with the natural world, and the profound understanding that even in solitude, the human spirit could endure. With each step, I embraced the unknown, eager to uncover the depths of my own resilience and the vast mysteries that lay ahead.

The Dance of Memories

In the depths of my solitary journey, memories became my closest companions. They emerged like ethereal wisps, dancing on the fringes of my consciousness, reminding me of the lives and moments that had once filled this world. Each memory carried a bittersweet weight, both a reminder of what was lost and a testament to the enduring power of the human spirit.

I sought solace in these memories, allowing them to envelop me like a familiar embrace. I would sit beneath the shade of a towering tree or beside a babbling brook, closing my eyes and allowing the echoes of the past to transport me to a time when laughter filled the air and bustling streets thrived with life.

I recalled the joy of family gatherings, the warmth of a lover's touch, and the shared experiences that wove the tapestry of human connection. Faces once familiar, now faded, materialised in my mind's eye. Their voices whispered through the wind, their laughter reverberating in the quiet corners of my heart.

In these moments of reflection, I discovered the power of nostalgia and its ability to bridge the gap between the past and the present. I allowed myself to feel the weight of loss, to grieve for the world that had been, and to honour the memories that shaped my existence.

With each memory, I wove a thread of gratitude for the experiences and connections that had shaped me. I revelled in the love shared, the lessons learned, and the moments of profound beauty that had imprinted themselves upon my soul. These memories became my sustenance, nourishing me in the depths of my solitude, reminding me of the richness of a life well-lived.

But as the days turned into weeks and the weeks into months, I realised that dwelling solely in the realm of memories was not enough. The dance of nostalgia, while comforting, could not be the sole purpose of my existence. I yearned for a sense of purpose that extended beyond the echoes of the past.

In my continued exploration of the post-apocalyptic world, I stumbled upon forgotten libraries, their shelves laden with volumes of knowledge and wisdom. I immersed myself in the written words of philosophers, poets, and thinkers who had shaped the course of human history. Their insights became a beacon of light in the darkness, guiding me towards a deeper understanding of myself and the world that surrounded me.

Armed with the power of knowledge, I began to cultivate a new purpose in my solitary existence. I sought to leave a mark on the world, however small it may be. I took up the brush and the pen, allowing my creativity to flow onto canvas and paper. I created art that spoke of resilience, hope, and the indomitable spirit of the human soul. I wrote stories that captured the essence of our shared humanity, preserving the collective memories that now resided within me.

I also embarked on acts of kindness, tending to the wounded creatures I encountered in the wilderness, nurturing injured birds back to health, and offering comfort to the orphaned animals that sought refuge in my presence. In these acts of compassion, I found purpose—a purpose rooted in the interconnectedness of all living beings, in the belief that even in solitude, we are bound by a shared responsibility to care for the world that remains.

And so, in the dance of memories and the pursuit of purpose, I forged a new path through the remnants of the post-apocalyptic world. I revelled in the nostalgia that whispered of what once was, but I also embraced the present, determined to make a difference in whatever ways I could. The echoes of the past would continue to guide me, but now they would serve as a backdrop to the unfolding chapters of my own unique story.

The Symphony of Resilience

In the wake of memories and the pursuit of purpose, I found myself drawn towards the remnants of human civilization that still echoed with whispers of life. It was as if the vestiges of our collective existence called out to me, urging me to explore further and uncover the stories that lay hidden within the ruins.

I ventured into once-thriving cities, their towering skyscrapers now mere skeletons of a bygone era. Broken windows reflected the passage of time, and graffiti adorned the walls like fragments of forgotten art. The streets, once bustling with the rhythm of human activity, now lay in a state of solemn stillness.

Within these urban labyrinths, I discovered remnants of resilience that defied the harsh reality of a world left behind. Community gardens sprouted defiantly amidst the cracked pavement, their vibrant blooms serving as symbols of hope and renewal. In the midst of desolation, makeshift shelters offered shelter to those who sought refuge.

In the heart of a dilapidated library, I stumbled upon a treasure trove of knowledge preserved in weathered books. Each page held the wisdom of the past, waiting to be rediscovered and shared. With reverence, I turned the pages, immersing myself in the tales of human triumph and resilience that had stood the test of time.

As I ventured deeper into the ruins, I encountered remnants of human ingenuity that left me in awe. Abandoned laboratories hinted at scientific breakthroughs, abandoned art studios revealed unfinished masterpieces, and remnants of technological marvels whispered of the progress we had achieved. The ghosts of human endeavour haunted these spaces, reminding me that even in the face of adversity, creativity and innovation had flourished.

With newfound purpose, I dedicated myself to uncovering and preserving the artefacts of our shared heritage. I meticulously catalogued the books, paintings, and remnants of technology, aiming to create a repository of knowledge that would endure beyond my own existence. It became my mission to honour the resilience of the human spirit and ensure that the achievements of our civilization would not be forgotten.

But it wasn't just the physical remnants of human civilization that intrigued me. As I ventured deeper into the abandoned cityscapes, I discovered the power of collective memory imprinted in the architecture itself. The buildings, monuments, and public spaces were witnesses to the stories of countless lives, and their silent presence whispered tales of triumph and tragedy.

In the evenings, as the sun dipped below the horizon, I would sit amidst the ruins, listening to the symphony of a world that had fallen silent. The wind carried echoes of laughter, footsteps, and conversations long gone. It was in these moments of stillness that I felt the weight of our shared humanity—the struggles, the joys, the dreams, and the resilience that had propelled us forward.

As I immersed myself in the remnants of human

civilization, I couldn't help but wonder about the possibilities of the future. In the absence of others, I became a guardian of our legacy, a steward of the stories that once animated these abandoned spaces. I knew that my time on this earth was finite, but the impact I could make, the seeds of resilience and hope I could sow, would endure far beyond my existence.

And so, in this chapter of my solitary existence, I became a curator of memories, a witness to the resilience of the human spirit. The remnants of a world gone by spoke volumes, reminding me that even in the face of overwhelming loss, the indomitable human capacity to rebuild, to create, and to forge connections would forever persist. And as I continued my journey through the post-apocalyptic landscape, I carried with me the symphony of resilience, hoping to inspire others who may one day venture forth and discover the echoes of our shared past.

Silent Whispers

As the seasons wove their tapestry of change, I found myself immersed in a world that seemed to pulsate with hidden energy. The vibrant greens of spring breathed new life into the landscapes, painting the meadows with a kaleidoscope of wildflowers. The warm embrace of summer bathed the earth in golden hues, while autumn adorned the trees with a fiery display of colours. And in the stillness of winter, a quiet serenity settled upon the land, blanketing it in a pristine coat of snow.

In this ever-changing tableau, I discovered that the natural world possessed an inherent resilience of its own. Amidst the ruins of human civilization, life found a way to persevere. Tender shoots broke through the cracks in concrete, and delicate vines crept along weathered walls, reclaiming the spaces that had once belonged to mankind. It was a reminder that life, in all its tenacity, could find a path forward even in the harshest of environments.

Inspired by the resilience of nature, I embarked on a mission to foster new life in this post-apocalyptic world. With seeds carefully collected from the remnants of once-thriving gardens, I began to cultivate small pockets of greenery amidst the desolation. Every plot of land, no matter how small, became a canvas for hope—a testament to the possibility of renewal and growth.

With each sunrise, I tended to these green oases, nurturing them with care and dedication. The simple act of planting seeds and watching them sprout into vibrant plants became a metaphor for my own journey—a reminder that even in the face of solitude, there was still room for growth and transformation.

The emergence of these small havens of life did not go unnoticed. Creatures, both great and small, began to seek refuge in these newfound sanctuaries. Birds sang their melodies from the branches of trees, and butterflies danced in graceful arcs, their delicate wings carrying the promise of metamorphosis. It was as if the natural world had sensed the whispers of hope and rallied around it, breathing life into the forgotten corners of this post-apocalyptic landscape.

As the gardens flourished, I expanded my efforts beyond nurturing flora. I sought out injured animals, using the knowledge gained from books and the guidance of my intuition to offer them solace and healing. With makeshift shelters and tender care, I tended to their wounds and watched as they regained strength, returning to the wilderness that had become their sanctuary.

Through these acts of compassion, I discovered the profound interconnectedness of all living beings. We were not isolated islands in a sea of solitude; we were part of a larger tapestry of life, bound by the fragile threads of existence. The presence of these creatures became a reminder that my role was not only to witness and preserve, but also to actively participate in the ongoing dance of life.

In the evenings, as I sat beneath the stars, a sense of peace settled upon me. The world may have been forever changed, but the spirit of resilience and the enduring beauty of the natural world continued to captivate my soul. I found solace in the symphony of crickets and the gentle rustle of leaves, knowing that even in the absence of human voices, there was still harmony to be found.

With each passing day, I became more attuned to the delicate balance of life in this post-apocalyptic world. The gardens I tended became a testament to the power of hope, reminding me that even in the face of devastation, there was room for renewal and growth. The whispers of hope, carried by the wind, echoed through the landscapes, inspiring me to embrace the possibilities that lay ahead.

And so, in this chapter of my solitary existence, I became a guardian of life—a steward of both the natural world and the resilience of the human spirit. Amidst the ruins and the remnants, I found a sense of purpose that transcended the boundaries of my solitude. In the quiet moments and the whispers of hope, I discovered the profound truth that even in the absence of others, the flame of resilience could be kept alive, illuminating the path towards a future yet to be written.

Its all the same

In the depths of my solitary existence, I had grown accustomed to the silence that enveloped the post-apocalyptic world. Days turned into weeks, and weeks into months, as I traversed the barren landscapes, leaving footprints as the only evidence of my presence. Yet, amidst the solitude, an undeniable longing for human connection continued to echo within me.

It was on a day like any other that I stumbled upon an abandoned village, nestled at the edge of a decaying forest. As I cautiously explored its crumbling streets and dilapidated houses, a peculiar sensation coursed through my veins—a feeling of being watched, as if unseen eyes were observing my every move.

Curiosity compelled me to investigate further, leading me to the remnants of a community centre. Inside, I discovered a collection of old photographs, preserved in dusty albums. The faces captured within the yellowed pages stared back at me, frozen in time, their eyes filled with a warmth that seemed to transcend the boundaries of the photographs themselves.

These photographs became a portal into the lives that once thrived within this forgotten village. I studied the faces, the gestures, and the shared moments frozen in time, yearning to know their stories. They were no longer strangers; they became a part of me, their memories intertwining with my own as if we had lived parallel lives in different eras.

Driven by a newfound sense of connection, I delved deeper into the village, exploring the remnants of homes and personal belongings left behind. Each item held a story—a worn teddy bear that spoke of childhood innocence, a well-used guitar that whispered melodies of forgotten songs, and letters inked with heartfelt words that carried the weight of love and longing.

In these relics of the past, I found solace. I realised that even though these individuals were no longer physically present, their essence lingered in the spaces they once inhabited. The empty streets came alive with their laughter, their conversations, and the indelible mark they left upon the world.

Inspired by the lingering presence of those who came before, I decided to honour their memory in a tangible way. I transformed the abandoned community centre into a sanctuary—a place where their stories would be preserved and shared. I carefully arranged the photographs, artefacts, and written words, creating an immersive experience that allowed visitors to step back in time, to immerse themselves in the lives and stories of the village's former inhabitants.

Word of the sanctuary spread, and gradually, other wanderers and survivors made their way to the village. Their arrival was a revelation—a confirmation that I was not alone in my quest for connection. These individuals, like me, carried the weight of a world lost, but they also carried a flicker of hope—a yearning for human connection that transcended the boundaries of solitude.

Together, we formed a small community—a gathering of souls united by a shared understanding and a shared desire to keep the echoes of humanity alive. We worked collectively to cultivate the gardens, restore crumbling structures, and breathe life into the forgotten spaces. It was as if, in the act of reviving the village, we were reviving ourselves—reconnecting with the essence of what it meant to be human.

In the evenings, as we sat around crackling fires, stories were shared—tales of survival, resilience, and the power of the human spirit. Each story wove another thread into the intricate tapestry of our collective existence, reminding us of our shared vulnerability, strength, and the undeniable beauty of human connection.

Through these connections, I discovered that even in a world stripped of its former glory, we could forge new bonds and create meaning. Our shared experiences, hopes, and dreams breathed life into the empty spaces, illuminating the darkness with a radiant light.

As the days turned into months and the months into years, our community flourished. The village became a beacon of resilience—a testament to the endurance of the human spirit. Our collective efforts transformed the forgotten remnants of the past into a living testament of our shared existence, a reminder that even in the face of utter devastation, connections could be forged and a sense of belonging could be found.

And so, in this phase of my solitary existence, I discovered that while I may have been the last person on earth, I was not alone in my journey. Through the echoes of connection, we built a community that defied the boundaries of time and space—a sanctuary where the past intertwined with the present, and where the whispers of the forgotten found solace in the hearts of those who remained.

Tapestry of Legacy

Within the embrace of our newfound community, the echoes of connection reverberated with a resounding strength. The village had become a haven of shared experiences, where the tapestry of our collective legacy continued to unravel and weave its intricate threads. As time passed, we recognized the importance of preserving not only our own stories but also the stories of those who came before us.

Together, we embarked on a mission to document the history of our world—a chronicle that would bridge the gap between the past and the present, ensuring that the legacy of humanity would endure. We gathered in the sanctuary, poring over the collections of photographs, artefacts, and written accounts, piecing together a narrative that spanned generations.

We formed a team of archivists, historians, and storytellers who painstakingly reconstructed the events leading up to the cataclysm that had reshaped our world. Through meticulous research and interviews with the elder members of our community, we unveiled the untold stories of bravery, sacrifice, and love that had shaped the course of our civilization.

As the years passed, our efforts bore fruit. The village became a repository of knowledge—a living testament to the resilience and triumphs of humanity. The sanctuary became a vibrant hub of learning and reflection, where visitors from far and wide came to immerse themselves in the tapestry of our shared history.

Beyond the physical records, we recognized the importance of passing down our stories through the oral tradition. We gathered around campfires, under the twinkling stars, and shared the tales of our experiences—the challenges we had faced, the lessons we had learned, and the hope that had sustained us. Each narrative became a part of the collective memory, etched into the hearts of future generations who would carry the torch of our legacy.

In addition to the preservation of our past, we sought to build a future that honoured the resilience of humanity. We expanded our community, reaching out to other isolated pockets of survivors who had found their own ways to persevere. Together, we shared knowledge, resources, and skills, pooling our strengths to rebuild what had been lost.

In the midst of our collective efforts, we discovered the power of collaboration and innovation. We utilised the remnants of technology, repurposing them to harness renewable energy sources, develop sustainable farming techniques, and establish communication networks. The post-apocalyptic world began to witness the re-emergence of progress—a testament to our determination to rise above the ashes of the past.

As the years turned into decades, our village grew and transformed. The once-dilapidated structures were rebuilt, harmonising with nature rather than overpowering it. Gardens flourished, providing sustenance and beauty, while renewable energy powered our communal spaces.

Our community became a shining beacon of resilience—a testament to what could be achieved when humanity worked together towards a common purpose.

But amidst our achievements, we never forgot the fragile balance of the world we now inhabited. We embraced our responsibility as stewards of the earth, nurturing its resources with reverence and care. We passed down the knowledge of sustainability and conservation to future generations, ensuring that our legacy would be one of harmony and respect for the world around us.

In the quiet moments of reflection, I marvelled at the transformation that had taken place. From the solitary existence I had once known, I had become a catalyst for the resurgence of hope and the preservation of our shared humanity. Together, we had created something beautiful— a testament to the indomitable spirit of humanity and the enduring power of connection.

As I gazed upon the village, vibrant with life and purpose, I realised that our story was not just a tale of survival; it was a story of resilience, unity, and the unwavering belief that even in the face of immense challenges, the human spirit could rise above, weaving a new tapestry of hope and possibility.

And so, in this chapter of our collective journey, we stood as guardians of our legacy—a testament to the indomitable spirit of humanity, forever committed to preserving the echoes of our past and crafting a future filled with boundless potential.